A CHRISTMAS CAROL

Written by **Charles Dickens**
Illustrations by **Pipi Sposito**

KB086161

스푼북

MARLEY'S GHOST

Let's begin at the beginning: Marley was dead. There could be no doubt about that. Yes, old Marley was as dead as a doornail.

Ebenezer Scrooge and Jacob Marley had been partners in business for many years. Scrooge was his only friend, and the only person at his funeral – apart from the priest, that is. Yet Scrooge was not very upset by this sad event. He even went to work on the day of Marley's funeral.

You see, Scrooge was a very greedy fellow! Business always came first. He was as hard and sharp as a piece of flint, and as cold, too. Even on the hottest days of summer, his glare sent icy shivers down your spine.

One Christmas Eve, old Scrooge sat busy in his office. It was cold, foggy weather. Yet Scrooge didn't shut the door of his office. He needed to keep an eye on his clerk, who was sitting in a miserable little room, copying out letters.

Scrooge had a small fire. It was so tiny that its heat barely left the fireplace. The clerk, whose name was Bob Cratchit, put on his white woollen scarf and tried to warm himself by the flame of his candle. It did not work.

'Merry Christmas, Uncle!' cried a cheerful voice. It was Scrooge's nephew, Fred.

'Bah!' said Scrooge. 'Humbug!'

'Don't be cross, Uncle!'

'If I had my way,' said Scrooge, 'every idiot who goes about with "Merry Christmas" on his lips, would be boiled with his own pudding, and buried with a stake of holly through his heart.'

'Don't be angry, Uncle,' said Fred. 'Come and dine with us tomorrow.'

Scrooge said that he would sooner see him in – well, in a place I'd rather not name. Despite all this, Fred remained cheerful. He wished his uncle and the clerk a merry Christmas as he left the office.

The final hour of work went very slowly. Finally, Scrooge nodded to the clerk that it was time to stop. Instantly Bob Cratchit snuffed out his candle and put on his hat.

'You'll want all day off tomorrow, I suppose?' said Scrooge. The next day was Christmas Day.

'If it's convenient, sir,' Bob Cratchit replied.

'It's not convenient,' Scrooge snapped. 'But I suppose you must have the whole day off. Be here earlier the next morning.'

Ebenezer Scrooge lived in a gloomy spot in a sad heap of a building. It was shut away in a courtyard off the street. The courtyard was so dark and foggy that even Scrooge, who knew every stone of the path, had to grope with his hands until he arrived at his door.

Scrooge rarely gave a single thought to Jacob Marley, his business partner who had been dead for seven years now. So why did Scrooge, with his key in his hand, see the door knocker transforming into the face of Jacob Marley?

The face was not angry or fierce. It looked at Scrooge in the way Marley used to look, eyes wide open. The hair shifted very slightly, as if blown a breeze that was not there.

Scrooge's blood ran cold. But he put his key in the keyhole, turned it firmly, walked in, and lit a candle. Out loud he shouted 'Bah!' Then, 'Humbug!'

He walked up the dark stairs.
When he reached his room, he
double-locked and bolted the door.
Then he checked under the table,
under the armchair and inside the
cupboards.

When he was sure he was quite alone, Scrooge put on his dressing-gown, slippers and nightcap, and sat down before a small fire.

There was a servant's bell near the fireplace. Scrooge did not keep any servants, so he was very surprised when the bell began to ring – all by itself.

From deep down below came a clanking noise, as if some person were dragging a heavy chain. It clanked up the stairs, and stopped outside his door.

Clank.

'It's humbug still!' said Scrooge.
'I won't believe it.'

Clank.

Clank.

The colour drained from Scrooge's
face. A shape was coming through

the door, without even opening it
first. As it came in, the dying flame
in the fire leapt up as if to cry out,
'I know him! It's Marley's ghost!'

The ghost's eyes were as cold
as death. A kind of bandage was

wrapped around the top of his head and chin. The chain he dragged was locked about his middle. It was long, and coiled around him like a tail. From it hung cash boxes, keys and padlocks, account books and heavy steel purses.

His body was transparent. Scrooge looked down at Marley's waistcoat and could see right through to the door behind him.

'What do you want with me?' said Scrooge, his voice shaking slightly.

'A great deal!' It was Marley's voice, no doubt about it.

'Why are you wearing a chain?' asked Scrooge, trembling now.

'I wear the chain that I created in my lifetime,' said the ghost. 'It is made of the things that mattered to me. Not other people, kindness or forgiveness, but cash boxes, purses and account books. It's terrible. You are wearing a similar chain yourself, Ebenezer Scrooge, though you cannot see it.'

Scrooge fell upon his knees and clasped his hands over his face.

'What should I do?' he wailed.

'I am here to warn you. You still have a chance and hope of escaping my fate. A chance and hope that I have gained for you, Ebenezer.'

'You were always a good friend to me,' said Scrooge.

'You will be haunted,' said the ghost, 'by three spirits. Expect to see the first tomorrow morning, when the bell tolls one o'clock.'

The ghost backed away from Scrooge. With every step he took, the window in the room raised itself

a little, so that when he reached it, it was wide open.

After the ghost vanished, Scrooge closed the window and examined the door by which the ghost had entered. It was still double-locked, and the bolts were undisturbed. He tried to say *Humbug!* but could not get beyond 'Hum'.

Whether it was because of the day's work, the ghost's grim words, or simply because it was late, Ebenezer Scrooge felt in need of rest. He went straight to his four-poster bed, pulled the curtains open and, without undressing, fell asleep at once.

THE FIRST OF THE THREE SPIRITS

When Scrooge awoke, he forgot for a moment everything that had happened to him. Then he heard the bell from the nearby church striking the hour.

Ding-dong!

One ring and no more.

One o'clock in the morning.

The exact time Marley's ghost had predicted ...

There was a sudden burst of light beside his bed. The curtains

surrounding it were drawn back on
one side.

Scrooge sat up and found himself
face to face with an unearthly
visitor. It was the size of a small
child and and had a smooth,
unwrinkled face. Yet its hair, which

hung down its back, was as white
as an old lady's.

'Who are you?' Scrooge
demanded.

'I am the Ghost of Christmas
Past,' the spirit said in a soft voice.
'Get up and walk with me.'

The spirit took him gently by the hand. To Scrooge's amazement, they passed through his bedroom wall and moments later were standing on an open country road. It was a clear winter day. Fresh snow covered the ground.

'Good Heaven!' cried Scrooge. 'I was brought up in this place. I was a boy here!'

They walked along the road. Scrooge knew every gate and post and tree. A little market town appeared in the distance, with a bridge, a church and a winding river.

Scrooge and the ghost turned down a lane and came to a red-brick mansion. He remembered it well. They walked through the solid wall, into a bare room. There they saw a small boy reading by a tiny fire.

Scrooge was startled to recognise himself. This was him as a boy, left alone at Christmas. But not completely alone. A girl entered the room.

She said: 'I have come to bring you home, dear brother!'

'Poor Fan,' said Scrooge, watching as his sister and his younger self climbed into the carriage that would take them both home. 'She died young.'

'But she had a child before she died?' said the ghost.

'Yes, my nephew Fred,' said Scrooge, feeling sorry that he had turned down Fred's invitation to Christmas dinner. He had been so rude to the young man.

Now the scene changed. The spirit took Scrooge through city streets, where the shops were lit up for Christmas. They finally stopped at the door of a warehouse.

'You know this place?' asked the ghost.

'Know it? I was an apprentice here. I worked for the owner, Mr Fezziwig. I learnt about business from him.'

Again, they glided inside without opening the door. Scrooge saw his younger self. He was with another young apprentice called Richard Wilkins.

Somehow it was Christmas Eve all over again. Old Scrooge saw Mr Fezziwig – always cheerful and generous – shut up shop early. He asked young Scrooge and Richard Wilkins to join him, his family and neighbours in the festive celebrations.

There was music from a fiddler. There was dancing, talk and laughter. There were cold roast meats, mince pies and warm mulled wine. Scrooge grew almost dizzy at the sight and sound and loveliness of it all.

He thought of how he had treated his clerk, Bob Cratchit, earlier that day. But his thoughts were disturbed when the spirit said: 'My time grows short. Quick!'

The scene changed again to show Ebenezer Scrooge, a little older now, with a beautiful young girl. Her eyes were sparkling with tears. They sat side by side, but it was as if there were an invisible wall between them.

Old Scrooge knew exactly what was about to happen. The young

Scrooge asked the girl, 'What has come between us, Belle?'

'You think only of money,' she said.

'Money makes you safe,' protested young Scrooge.

'You are not the man you were when we were younger and poorer,' said Belle. 'I could not make you happy now. Only money can do that. I hope you are happy with the life you have chosen!'

The woman got up and left the room.

'I have seen enough, spirit,' said old Scrooge. 'Don't torment me any longer.'

'One more scene,' said the ghost.

Next they were invisible guests
at a different house, watching a
mother sitting by the fire. Scrooge
recognised her. She was older but
still beautiful. Children played
and ran around her. A man came
into the room, laden with toys and
presents. Christmas again!

The children squealed with joy
as they greeted their father and his
presents. Then he, too, sat down by
the fire.

'Belle,' said the husband, turning
to his wife with a smile. 'I saw an
old friend of yours this afternoon.'

'Who was it?'

'Mr. Scrooge. I passed his office window. There he sat, all alone. I think he is quite alone in the world.'

'Spirit,' said old Scrooge to the ghost. 'Take me away from here. I cannot bear it.'

Suddenly, Scrooge found himself alone and back in his own bedroom. He was exhausted from his ghostly trip, and was full of sorrow and regret. He barely had time to stagger to bed before he sank into a heavy sleep.

The Second of the Three Spirits

When Ebenezer Scrooge next awoke, something strange was happening. Two strange things, in fact.

The church clock was striking.

Ding-dong!

One ring.

One o'clock.

Again.

As if he had travelled back in time.

And once again there was a light outside his bed curtains. This time it was a warm glow.

Scrooge got out of bed. The light was coming from the next room. It was the fire, a bigger, warmer fire than the fireplace had ever contained. The walls were hung with crisp leaves of holly, mistletoe and ivy. Heaped everywhere were turkeys, geese, chickens, long strings of sausages, mince pies, plum puddings, shiny chestnuts, red apples, juicy oranges,

luscious pears, and steaming bowls
of mulled wine.

In the middle of all this plenty sat
a jolly giant, wearing a green robe.

'I am the Ghost of Christmas
Present,' said the spirit.

By now Scrooge knew what to expect. When the spirit told him to grasp hold of the green robe, he did so.

The next moment they were in a city street piled with snow. It was daytime and people were cheerfully clearing the snow from their steps. Christmas was in the air.

They passed shop windows crammed with a whole alphabet of delicious foods and drinks, including apples and almonds, baked bread, cinnamon and coffee. Then they found themselves outside the little house belonging to Scrooge's clerk, Bob Cratchit.

Scrooge and the Ghost of Christmas Present passed silently through the closed door. They stood in a corner watching Mrs Cratchit and her family preparing Christmas dinner. It was to be goose with sage and onion stuffing. A Christmas pudding was steaming away on the hob.

When the food was almost ready,
Bob Cratchit came home from church.

He carried his son, Tiny Tim, on his back. Tim could barely walk, even with his crutch. But he was as happy as the rest of the family when they tucked into their goose, chatting and laughing.

'A merry Christmas to us all, my dears,' said Bob to his family. 'God bless us!'

'God bless us, every one!' echoed Tiny Tim.

'We should drink to Mr Scrooge,' said Bob. 'Thank you, Mr Scrooge, for paying my wages so that I could afford this delicious feast.'

'You're thanking Mr Scrooge?' cried Mrs. Cratchit. 'I wish I had him here. I'd give him a piece of my mind to feast upon for treating you so badly.'

Scrooge, standing invisible in the corner, was ashamed to see how the mere mention of his name seemed

to cast a gloom over the Cratchits.

They were not a handsome, well-dressed family. But they were happy and grateful and contented with their life. As Scrooge left with the spirit, he had his eye upon them, and especially on Tiny Tim, until the last.

Outside, it was snowing again.

'Think how this day is being celebrated everywhere,' said the Ghost of Christmas Present. 'In the most distant villages, even in lighthouses and on ships out at sea. And closer to home, too.'

Now Scrooge and the spirit were inside another home. This one was much larger than the one they had just visited. After a moment, Scrooge recognised his nephew and his pretty wife. Fred's wife's sisters were there and other guests as well. Fred was laughing. He was telling a story. It was a story about Scrooge.

'He said that Christmas was humbug. He believed it too!
He turned down my invitation to dine with us, as he always does.
But I'm going to give him the same chance every year, whether he likes it or not.'

'Why?' someone asked.

'Because I feel sorry for him,' said Fred.

There was music and singing in this house, too. After dinner, they played games like blindman's bluff and another one called 'Yes and No'. In this game, Scrooge's nephew thought of something. Everyone else had to find out what it was, with

Fred only answering their questions with "yes" or "no".

Fred said he was thinking of an animal – a rather *unfriendly* animal. An animal that growled and grunted sometimes, talked sometimes, lived in London, and walked the streets. No, it wasn't a horse, or a cow, or a bull, or a tiger, or a dog, or a pig, or a cat.

'I know what it is, Fred,' said one of Fred's wife's sisters. 'It's your Uncle Scrooge!'

At this, they all laughed. Yet they still drank a toast to Scrooge. The old man was touched, standing unseen in the room.

It was time to move again. Scrooge and the spirit left Fred's house.

Scrooge noticed that the spirit looked much older suddenly. As if it could read his mind, the spirit said: 'My life upon this earth is very brief. It ends tonight at midnight, when this Christmas Day ends.'

The church bell struck twelve.

Scrooge looked for the ghost,
but it had gone. As the last stroke of
twelve faded away, he saw a solemn,
hooded, ghostly creature, moving
like a mist towards him.

The Third of The Three Spirits

The third ghost approached slowly and silently. It wore a deep black cloak that covered its head, that covered its body, that covered everything except its outstretched hand.

Scrooge almost fell to his knees in fright. He said in a trembling voice:

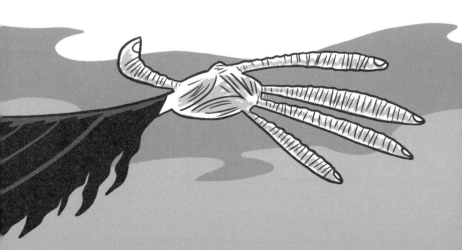

'You are the Ghost of Christmas Yet to Come. You are about to show me things that have not yet happened.'

The shrouded head of the figure seemed to nod. Then Scrooge was swept away in the shadow of its

cloak. They came to the heart of
the city, near the Stock Exchange,
where businessmen worked.

The ghost's hand pointed to a group of businessmen. They were talking.

'I don't know much about it, either way,' said a man with a large chin. 'I only that know he's dead.'

'When did he die?' asked another.

'Last night, I believe.'

'What has he done with his money?' asked a red-faced gentleman.

'I haven't heard,' said the man with the large chin. 'All I know is that he hasn't left it to me. And it's likely to be a very cheap funeral. He had no friends, so I don't know of anybody who will go to it.'

The men laughed and strolled away.

Who were they talking about? Scrooge wondered. Who had died? It couldn't be old Jacob Marley, for he died seven years ago. This spirit was showing him things that hadn't happened yet.

The spirit whisked him away to a poorer part of town, to a broken-down shop full of junk. All around them were things like old bottles and threadbare blankets, rusty keys and hinges.

A woman came into the junk shop and produced a roll of dark material.

'What's this?' said the gruff, pipe-smoking man behind the counter.

'Bed curtains,' said the woman. 'Don't worry. They're not mine. The owner's dead. I took 'em down while he was still lying there. Here's some blankets and a shirt of his, too. How much will you give me for the lot?'

Scrooge never heard the answer. Instead, the spirit transported him to the bed itself, standing bare without its curtains. A shape lay stretched out on it, beneath a ragged sheet.

Who was under the sheet?

He thought he knew, but did not want to believe it.

Scooge turned to the spirit, who was still hovering nearby: 'Is there any person who is sad about this man's death?'

Another scene unfolded before them. A woman with children, anxiously waiting for her husband to return home.

A young man burst through the door. The wife said. 'Is the news good or bad?'

Scrooge recognised the young man. He was one of the many people Scrooge had lent money to. A large sum of money. Money to be paid back on time and without any excuses.

The husband said nothing.

'Will he show us any mercy?' asked the woman. 'Will he give us more time to pay him back?'

'He cannot give us more time,' said her husband. 'He is dead.'

Ebenezer Scrooge saw the woman smile, just slightly and only for an

instant.

Then she seemed to grow ashamed at being glad of another person's death because it freed them from debt.

Scrooge had his answer: people weren't sad that this man was dead, some were even *pleased*.

The scene changed once more. Now they were near Scrooge's office, the one he had once shared with Jacob Marley. The spirit pointed to the window. Scrooge hurried to look in.

He didn't recognise the furniture inside. He didn't recognise the person inside, either.

Lastly, they arrived at an overgrown graveyard. The spirit pointed to a gravestone.

'Before I draw nearer to that gravestone,' said Scrooge, 'answer me one question. Are the things you have shown me the shadows of what

will happen? Or are they only the shadows of what *may* happen?'

Still, the ghost kept silent and pointed to the grave. Scrooge crept towards it, trembling as he went.

Following the direction of the finger, he read the name upon the stone of the neglected grave: Ebenezer Scrooge.

Scrooge tried to grab at the ghostly hand beside him.

'I am not the man I was,' he pleaded. 'Allow me another chance and I will be a better man. I will honour Christmas in my heart and try to be kind and merry all the year. Anything to avoid the future you have shown me.'

Scrooge saw a change in the its hood and dress. It shrank and turned into a bedpost.

His own bedpost.

He was home again.

The End
of It

Yes, the bedpost was his own, the bed was his own and the room was his own.

Best of all, he was alive.

Scrooge was being given another chance!

He would be a better man.

Running to the window, he threw it open and leaned out. No fog, no mist. It was a clear, bright, sunny morning.

'What day is it?' asked Scrooge, calling down to a boy outside.

'Today?' replied the boy. 'Why, it's Christmas Day!'

'It's Christmas Day!' said Scrooge to himself. 'I haven't missed it. The spirits have done it all in one night. They can do anything they like. Of course they can. Hello, down there.'

'Hello!' returned the boy.

Scrooge told the boy to run to the butcher's shop in the next street and buy the biggest turkey they had. When it arrived, Scrooge wrote down Bob Cratchit's address. He told the boy to deliver the turkey to his clerk's house. Scrooge paid for all this, and he was happy to be generous.

He went out into the streets and said 'Good morning!' and 'Happy Christmas!' to everyone he met. He was surprised to find how much happier he had become.

He even plucked up the courage
to go to his nephew Fred's. He
decided that he would join them
for dinner after all. Fred and his
family were pleased to see Scrooge
and he was pleased to see them.

They talked and laughed and sang together. It was just like the scene that Scrooge had witnessed with the second spirit. Except this time he was not invisible in a corner, and he was not full of regret.

The next day was Boxing Day. Scrooge arrived at his office very early. Bob Cratchit was not yet at work.

When the clerk did appear, Scrooge, who was sitting on the stool in his office, growled: 'What time of day do you think this is? You're late!'

'I am very sorry, sir,' said Bob. 'I am only a little late.'

'Only a *little* late!' Scrooge snapped. 'I am not going to stand for this sort of thing any longer.'

Bob started to tremble.

'Yes, things are going to change,' said Scrooge, leaping up from his stool.

He poked Bob in the ribs so hard that he staggered back. 'I am going to pay you more!'

Bob was too startled to reply.

'A merry Christmas, Bob!' said Scrooge, as he clapped him on the back. 'A merrier Christmas, my good fellow, than I have ever given you! I'll raise your salary and try to help your struggling family. First of all, though, light the fire, would you? Let's warm this place up!'

Scrooge was as good as his word. No, he wasn't as good as his word – he was better. He did it all and much more. To Tiny Tim he became like a second father, and a friend to the whole Cratchit family.

In fact, he became a better friend, a better employer and a better man

than you would ever imagine.

He was visited by no more ghosts of Christmas, from the past, present or future. And it was known far and wide that Ebenezer Scrooge was a man who knew how to celebrate Christmas the right way – with love, laughter and generosity.

May that be said of all of us!

And so, as Tiny Tim said: *God bless us, every one*!

Charles Dickens

Charles Dickens was born in Portsmouth in 1812. Like many of the characters he wrote about, his family were poor and his childhood was difficult. As an adult, he became known around the world for his books. He is remembered as one of the most important writers of his time.

Illustrations by
Pipi Sposito

Pipi Sposito was born in Buenos Aires. He's always been painting. As a child, he enjoyed making figures out of building clay, and when he was older, he started designing for humor magazines. He was surrounded by the original paintings of many experimental artists, and he painted various styles out of curiosity. His illustrated books include 《A Christmas Carol》《A Tale of Two Cities》《Great Expectations》《Oliver Twist》.

A CHRISTMAS CAROL

초판 1쇄 발행 2023년 6월 27일

글 찰스 디킨스 | 그림 피피 스포지토

ISBN 979-11-6581-429-8 (74840)
ISBN 979-11-6581-418-2 (세트)

발행처 주식회사 스푼북 | 발행인 박상희 | 총괄 김남원
편집 김선영·박선정·김선혜·권새미 | 디자인 조혜진·김광휘 | 마케팅 손준연·이성호·구혜지
출판신고 2016년 11월 15일 제2017-000267호
주소 (03993) 서울시 마포구 월드컵북로 6길 88-7 ky21빌딩 2층
전화 02-6357-0050(편집) 02-6357-0051(마케팅)
팩스 02-6357-0052 | 전자우편 book@spoonbook.co.kr

제품명 A Christmas Carol
제조자명 주식회사 스푼북 | 제조국명 대한민국 | 전화번호 02-6357-0050
주소 (03993) 서울시 마포구 월드컵북로6길 88-7 ky21빌딩 2층
제조년월 2023년 6월 27일 | 사용연령 8세 이상
※ KC마크는 이 제품이 공통안전기준에 적합하였음을 의미합니다.

⚠주 의

아이들이 모서리에 다치지
않게 주의하세요.